Dead Money

Graveside Reads Vol 1, Issue 2

D.L. Winchester

Undertaker Books

For my church camp poker buddies.

DEAD
MONEY

1

I PEEKED AT THE two cards lying face down in front of me, afraid they'd changed in the minute since I'd last checked them.

It was still a pair of aces: hearts and clubs.

The ace of spades was lying face up in the center of the table, along with the ace of diamonds and three queens. After three weeks of losing hands, my luck was finally turning, and just in time. The chips stacked in front of me were all I had left, my total net worth.

"Your bet," the dealer, a native woman of about forty, nodded at the man to her left. He was a large man, with a full head of white hair, wearing an expensive black suit. An orange pocket square was tucked in his jacket pocket, matching the tie he wore. His sunglasses probably cost more than my car was worth, and he had a small gold ring in his right ear.

Next to him sat a recreational gambler, probably from somewhere in the Carolina mountains. He played okay, but his tells were a little too obvious for even a serious amateur.

Between him and me was a gambler I'd crossed paths with before, Jack Kendall. Now on his fourth wife, he gambled to stay out of the house, moving up and down the east coast in an RV, trying to stay ahead of alimony and divorce lawyers.

But Jack and the other man had folded, leaving me and the sharp dresser.

He didn't even peek at his cards before sliding his entire pile of chips forward. "All in."

I let my poker face slip as I slid my own pile into the pot. "Call."

The dealer did some counting, and slid a few of my opponent's chips back to him to balance the wagers. It was well after midnight on the Quallah boundary, in a casino run by the Eastern Band of Cherokee Indians. The casino was small, made up mostly of slot machines and video poker, but there were a few tables for card games.

This late, our table and a nearby blackjack table were the only ones still playing.

The snappy dresser shook his head. He'd told us his name when he sat down, but I'd forgotten already. It was irrelevant; I'd probably never face him again. "I'm afraid you're not going to like this," he said. He flipped over his cards, revealing the king and queen of hearts. "My happy couple gives me four queens."

I grinned. "Actually, I do like it. Because while I'm partial to the ladies..." I flipped my cards. "I seem to be coming up aces."

He pulled off his sunglasses and stared at my cards, almost as if he was willing them to change.

They didn't.

Finally, he shook his head and chuckled as I pulled in the pot. If my math was right, I was around fifty-thousand dollars richer, and no longer in danger of running out of money.

I picked a five-hundred-dollar chip out of the pile and tipped the dealer before stacking my winnings in a tray. "I believe with that, I'll call it a night."

The snappy dresser nodded. "I probably should too." He shook his head. "Four fuckin' aces. I figured you'd fold as soon as I went all in."

"I guess you can't trust the ladies, can you?" I stood and picked up my tray.

"In my experience," the dealer cut in with a smile, "men aren't much better."

Five minutes after I made it to my room, there was a knock at the door. I figured it was Jack, come to talk shop and steal what he could from the mini-bar. But when I opened the door, it was a man in a hotel polo.

He held out an envelope. "Message for you, sir."

Reaching in my pocket, I took out a ten-dollar chip and gave it to him. I tried to keep some small chips handy for hotel staff. They were good sources of information: who was playing in the casino, what kind of streak they were on, if there were any upcoming tournaments with large pots. It never hurt to have them on your side.

Closing the door, I opened the envelope and found a note written on hotel stationary.

Before you turn in, will you have a drink with me? Black Bear Bar.

Folding the note, I tossed it in the trash and checked the time. It was late, but not too late for a nightcap.

\#

Casinos never sleep, though parts of them do slow down at times. There was one bartender at the Black Bear, serving a lone customer at the end of the bar. He was a tall, skinny man, in a suit that looked like it cost even more than my opponent's had. On his right pinkie was a large gold ring with an emerald mounted in it.

That ring probably cost enough to cover a month of bad luck, I decided. It was gaudy, but the expensive sort of gaudy, not the kind trying to hide defects behind ostentation.

"Evening," I said, sitting down next to him.

Up close, I saw he was young, probably young enough that the bartender had carded him. He had gray eyes, a narrow nose, and thin lips. A gambler of some kind, I decided, though I'd never seen him before.

"Evening," he said. "What'll you have?"

"Bourbon and branch," I told the bartender. "Knob Creek 12 year, if you have it."

I knew he had it, and I knew it was expensive. But I wanted to see if this young buck was all flash and no substance.

The bartender glanced at him, and he nodded. "I'll take another too."

He didn't say anything else until the drinks were in front of us. As the bartender walked away, I picked up my drink and took a sip. "I'm Sam Lytle. What'd you want to chat about?"

He took a toothpick from his pocket and twirled it back and forth between his fingers. "My name is Andy Whitmer. I represent a man named Alex Ford."

I shrugged. "Never heard the name."

Andy smiled. "I'd be surprised if you had. Mr. Ford is wealthy, wealthier than some nations, if you can believe that, but also not one to flaunt his wealth. He puts a lot of effort into remaining out of the public eye."

"As interesting as his money is, I'm not sure how it relates to me," I said, taking another sip.

Whitmer took a sip of his own drink. He had an energy around him, a strange excitement about what this conversation would lead to. Money covers a lot of sin, but it can't buy poise, the ability to hide your emotions no matter the circumstance.

"On occasion, Mr. Ford organizes a poker tournament with a few of his friends. Each of them selects someone to play on their behalf, and they wager on the outcome."

I nodded. "Sounds like something a rich man would do."

"The next tournament begins tomorrow," Whitmer said. "After watching you play tonight, Mr. Ford has instructed me to invite you to represent him."

I took another sip of my drink, buying time before I answered. Andy was uncomfortable, and I wondered if by waiting, I could draw out additional information.

Whitmer didn't volunteer anything, instead taking a gulp of his drink and signaling the bartender for another. I waited for the bartender, and in addition to Whitmer's drink, he placed a new one next to my half-empty glass.

"I assume the stakes are high?" I finally asked.

"The highest," Whitmer replied. "And the competition is fierce."

"I'm curious how Mr. Ford was able to watch me play tonight."

A smile. "There's always someone watching when you gamble."

I nodded agreement. Casinos are loaded with cameras, and every player and table is covered. It would be a simple matter for someone with Mr. Ford's money to gain access. "So why me? I'm sure you and Mr. Ford know I've had some bad luck recently."

"Because runs happen to everyone. What impressed Mr. Ford is how you acted when your luck changed. You played with patience and discipline, and came out with a pile of money as a result."

I nodded, appreciating the answer. "Is there a buy-in for this tournament?"

"Taken care of," Whitmer promised. "Five nights of poker in a luxury home with anything you can ask for. It'll be the best week of your career."

It felt like I was holding a nine with the ten and face cards on the table. I had a chance at something good, but the ace, the kicker, was still out there to give me a moment's pause.

After a moment, I decided to push my doubt aside and raised my glass.

"To winning a poker tournament!"

Whitmer smiled as he raised his in response.

2

Aﬀer checking out of the casino the next afternoon, I left the town behind and followed a winding road up a mountain.

The Qualla Boundary, home of the Cherokee in western North Carolina, is nestled in one of the most beautiful parts of the state. The Great Smoky Mountains National Park borders it to the north and west, its millions of visitors providing tourism revenue to the tribe.

The Qualla Cherokee had a reservation here due to the actions of a man named Will Thomas. A white man, he grew up near the Cherokee and befriended them. After being adopted by a chief, he continued working with the tribe while studying to become a lawyer. In time, Thomas became an Indian agent, and eventually, a Cherokee chief.

When President Andrew Jackson tried to evict the Cherokee from their ancestral home along the Trail of Tears, Thomas negotiated on behalf of the Qualla Cherokee, who had separated from the rest of the band. Thomas helped purchase the land that would become the Qualla Boundary, and eventually the Eastern Cherokee Reservation.

Thomas is also a footnote to history. As the commander of the Thomas Legion of the Confederate Army, his troops (which included Cherokee companies) were responsible for firing some of the last shots of the Civil War at Waynesville, just outside the reservation.

As I drove up the mountain road, I could see Waynesville in the distance.

Few gamblers know or care about that kind of history, but as a man who learned my trade playing in Native-owned casinos, I feel like it's important to learn about the history of the tribes I enrich. I spend most of my time among Natives, in the casino hotels and restaurants, and of course with the ones who work as dealers. After years of them being screwed by the white man, I decided if I was going to spend my time among them, I needed to understand as much about them as I could.

Brown and orange leaves covered the road, and I was glad the tournament was now. Once winter came, getting up this mountain in my ten-year-old car would be a real pain in the ass.

At the top of the mountain, the road ended at a metal gate set in a stone wall. A man in a black polo and khakis stood at each side of the road. One was balding, his close-cut dark hair receding across his scalp. He stepped toward my car while his partner, a younger man with a shaved head, held back.

"May I help you?"

The accent wasn't local. I didn't even think it was American. Maybe Eastern European, though I supposed it didn't matter. "My name is Sam Lytle," I said, holding out a hand. The man didn't shake it.

"Follow the driveway to the house. Someone will be there to greet you."

He stepped back, and the gate opened.

For a moment, fear caught me. I didn't know what was waiting down that road through the trees, but I could turn around and go back to the casino without finding out, maybe even move on to a new casino.

But then I remembered Whitmer's promise of life-changing rewards at no risk to my purse. With that in mind, I took my foot off the brake and drove up the tree-lined driveway.

Rounding a bend, the house appeared in front of me.

Well, it wasn't a house. It was a cabin, but it was huge. The center portion stretched to the sky, a massive A-frame with windows filling the ends. On both sides were lower structures, with log walls and an occasional window. It reminded me of a church.

And the altar would be a poker table.

I parked my car in the curved drive, taking my bag from the backseat. Another guard was standing by the door, and I wondered why they needed so much security.

Three other cars were parked in front of mine, along with two dark vans. I walked past them to the door, and the guard nodded to me.

"Hello, Mr. Lytle. Your suite is the second on the right. Ms. Po will open the game at eight o'clock.

I looked at my watch and saw it was approaching six. Two hours. "Thank you."

"My pleasure."

I walked through the glass front door. It was twelve feet tall and at least two inches thick, but so well balanced, I could have pushed it open with my pinkie.

Inside, the luxury continued. The furniture was meant to resemble a rustic hunting lodge, but I could tell the woods and leathers were far more expensive than an average hunter could afford.

Only one chair was occupied, and the man sitting in it jumped up when he saw me.

"Sam! You're here too?" Jack Kendall approached, extending his arms for a hug. I tolerated it, knowing he was trying to imply I was a valued friend.

The gamesmanship was starting early.

"I guess," I replied.

Jack smiled. "Well, don't take it personally when I win. I've got another divorce lawyer to pay."

I shook my head. "Number four didn't work out, huh?"

He chuckled. "Sure didn't. Apparently her favorite part about being married to a gambler was how often I was out of town so she could entertain gentlemen callers."

"Maybe if you spent more time at home," I suggested, earning another chuckle.

"Funny, you sound just like her." Jack raised an eyebrow. "Want to be wife number five?"

Now it was my turn to laugh. "I look like shit in heels."

A shake of his head. "Well, damn."

"I'm going to get settled in before the poker starts," I told him.

"Go ahead. Everyone else is in their suites. This place is fucking huge. And comfortable! I haven't been in a bed this nice since my second honeymoon." Jack winked. "I'd like to do the things I did on my second honeymoon in it, if you get my drift."

"You're not my type, Jack." I said, heading toward the hall to the right.

I found my suite, and it was as big as Jack promised. It had a full kitchen, with food in the cabinets and refrigerator, a living area with a comfortable couch across from a massive television, and off the living area, the bedroom and bath. I peeked in the bath and saw a jacuzzi tub almost big enough to swim in.

Awesome.

Tossing my bag on the bed, I stripped off my clothes and headed for the bathroom. An hour and a half later, I emerged, relaxed and primed for the evening ahead.

I could get used to this.

There was a minibar in the living room, with full bottles of whiskey, vodka, tequila, rum, and bourbon. I poured myself a bourbon and branch, noting it was the same bourbon I'd ordered in the bar the night before. The other liquors were also top shelf.

After enjoying my drink, I dressed for the night in jeans and a black t-shirt with a calavera on it. A dab of cologne and my sunglasses, and I was ready to play.

3

THE POKER TABLE WAS set on the opposite end of the room from the door, looking out over the valley below. Five chairs circled it, with stacks of chips in front of each chair.

I was the first to arrive, and I took my preferred seat, to the dealer's right. It meant I couldn't see out the windows behind me, but I didn't mind. Floodlights were on, limiting the view to the cabin's backyard. Taking off my sunglasses, I sat them on the table in front of me.

A few minutes later, Jack entered the room, followed by a young woman. She had shoulder-length blonde hair, and wore a tank top that exposed her generous bosom. When she saw me, she winked, and took the seat across from the dealer. Jack took the seat to her right.

She leaned across the table, extending a hand and giving me a long view of her cleavage. "I'm Megan."

I made a point of looking away from her tits as I took her hand and shook it. "Sam. Nice to meet you."

Another player joined us, a gray-haired man I'd seen a couple times at the Quallah casino, but had never shared a table with. He was dressed in a suit, with fancy aviator sunglasses.

"Bob Sunnell," he said, not offering to shake hands as he took the seat between me and Megan.

"I wonder which of you will get second place," Jack asked, leaning back in his chair.

Megan pretended to laugh. "You're funny." She put a hand on Jack's arm, and I saw him grin. He wasn't just expecting to leave here with the jackpot, he had his eye on wife number five too.

Fucker.

I quietly counted the chips in the stack in front of me. Twelve twenty-fives, eight fifties, and three hundreds. A thousand, in total.

Another woman came in, her Asian features making her age hard to guess, but I figured late thirties. She was in a t-shirt and jeans like me, the t-shirt containing letters in a language I didn't recognize. She took the seat next to the dealer.

"Hello everyone," she said. "I'm your host, Po Daiyu."

The rest of us nodded greetings.

"You've been selected to represent others in a game of poker. These men enjoy the skill of the game at its highest level, but do not tolerate cheating. It will be punished by immediate disqualification."

She paused, staring each of us in the eye before continuing.

"This is my fourth tournament hosting as the representative of Ahmed Bin Sallah. Should one of you win, you'll take my place as host."

Daiyu smiled, a challenge, but behind the smile, I could see something else, a tiredness.

"You must be very rich, to have already won three times," Megan said.

Daiyu shook her head. "The prize is worth it, but it's not something you can put in a bank account."

"I don't understand," Jack said. "The guy who invited us here, Whitmer, he said we're playing for the highest stakes?"

"You are," Daiyu said. "You're playing for your lives."

"What?" I heard myself blurt out as Jack pushed his chair back from the table.

"I've heard enough," he said as he stood. "I'm leaving."

Two of the guards entered, carrying assault rifles.

"Sit down," one of them ordered.

Jack opened his mouth to argue, but the guards raised their guns and he returned to his seat.

"This is kidnapping," Sunnell said. "Kidnapping and murder."

"It's entertainment," Daiyu replied. "Though your sponsors are watching, none of them are physically here. This home is rented by a shadow corporation controlled by one of the sponsors."

"I'm calling the police," Sunnell said, pulling a phone from his pocket. I was surprised when none of the guards moved to stop him.

Sunnell looked at the phone, then slammed it onto the table. "No fucking service!"

I saw a tear follow from Megan's eye. "Please. Don't do this. I have a kid, his health isn't good..."

"You don't have a kid," Daiyu said. "You ran away from home four years ago to a brothel in Nevada. When you had enough of the johns, you learned to play poker."

Megan's jaw dropped.

"They know us," I said, looking at Daiyu. "Someone did their research. Poker players are transient by nature. If someone goes missing, everyone assumes they moved on to another casino. I'd bet none of us have anyone to miss us. By the time someone notices we've disappeared, four of us will be dead."

The last word hung in the air as Daiyu nodded. "That's right. The sponsors have been doing this for almost two decades. As long as they keep moving the games, never pulling players from the same casinos too often, no one notices."

"Why can't we escape?" Jack asked. "You know the secrets, we can overpower the guards and make a run for it. One of us is bound to make it."

Daiyu shook her head. "There's a dozen guards on duty at a time. Besides, if you try to escape, they won't kill you. They'll bring you back and force you to play."

"How?" Sunnell asked.

Daiyu put a small case on the table and opened it. Inside was a leather collar with metal studs attached to a small box. Next to the collar was a remote.

"A shock collar?" Jack asked, leaning to look in the box.

"We're not dogs," Sunnell said.

"It doesn't matter," Daiyu said. "This is just one of the tools at their disposal. Believe me, you will play. All resisting will do is wear you out."

I leaned back in my chair, wishing I hadn't accepted the offer to join this table. But it sounded like it was too late for regrets.

Looking across the table, I could see the emotion in the other players' eyes. Jack and Bob were angry, and I understood that. I was having some of the same feelings myself. Megan was scared, her posture slipped and her eyes darting around, begging for an escape. Daiyu was indifferent. After participating in so many tournaments, I guessed her emotions had been overwhelmed.

"So what happens when we run out of chips?" I asked.

"You die," Daiyu said. "Each round has a different way of departure for the loser. Once someone has departed, play is paused and resumes the next night."

"What's the method of execution tonight?" Jack asked. "Firing squad? Boiled in oil? Iron Maiden?"

Daiyu shook her head. "Flight."

"Flight?" Megan asked.

Daiyu turned and pointed outside at the cliff edge. "Flight."

4

For a moment, we all stared out the window in silence. Then Sunnell slapped his hand on the table.

"Fuck it, let's get this show on the road. No sense sitting around wishing we could change things."

Daiyu nodded, and a new woman entered. She was older, gray hair pulled into a ponytail, with black slacks and a black vest over a white shirt.

Walking to the dealer position, she picked up a token marked "dealer" and put it in front of Daiyu.

"Dealer's choice," Daiyu explained. "Texas hold 'em, Five card draw, or Five card stud. Ante is always twenty-five, and is required."

The dealer took a deck of cards from a shelf beneath the table. Breaking the seal, she began to shuffle as we each tossed a white twenty-five chip into the pot.

"The game is Draw poker," Daiyu announced.

The dealer burned a card, then dealt five times around the table. I picked up my hand and studied it. A pair of jacks, a king, a nine, and a four.

"Your bet," the dealer said to Jack.

He rapped his knuckles on the table. "I'll call."

"Same." Megan rapped the felt surface, too.

Sunnell didn't even look at his cards before pushing his pile of chips into the pot. "I'm all in."

Megan gasped as Jack shook his head. I studied Sunnell for a moment, wondering what he was playing at. Did he have an edge, a secret I didn't know? Or was this his way to protest the situation he had found himself in, to put his fate in the hands of cards lest his skill end up killing someone?

Laying my cards face down, I pushed my chips into the pot as well. "Call the bet."

"Come on, be reasonable," Jack said, looking from me to Sunnell.

"This is reasonable," Sunnell replied. "Far more reasonable than playing to kill each other."

Daiyu tossed her cards onto the table. "I fold."

Jack looked down at his hand, shook his head again, and laid his cards down. "Fold."

Megan looked at the pile of chips on the table, and I could tell she was tempted. That many chips, this early in the game would be a huge advantage, especially if two other players would be eliminated.

Jack put his hand on her arm. "Don't do it. Don't be a fool."

She nodded, looked at the pot again, then laid her cards down. "Fold."

The dealer looked at Sunnell. "How many?"

He shook his head. Sunnell was standing with the five cards he'd been dealt, still unseen. There could be four aces in his hand, or nine-high nothing. We wouldn't know until the reveal.

"Two," I said, laying a pair of cards face down on the table. I was keeping the jacks and king.

The dealer burned a card, then dealt me two. I picked them up, and saw I'd come up with another king and the ace of spades.

At least I knew Sunnell didn't have four aces.

Reaching out, Sunnell flipped his cards over, revealing a pair of sixes, an ace, an eight, and a two.

I paused, looking around the table.

"Well?" Jack asked.

I laid my cards on the table and looked Sunnell in the eye. "Have a nice flight."

For a moment, the room was silent.

"Fuck!" Megan said. "My three threes would have beaten that!"

Sunnell was quiet, almost stoic. Behind him, I saw three guards enter the room.

"Well." He got to his feet. "I suppose this is goodbye."

I extended my hand, but he ignored it, turning and walking to the door leading outside as the guards followed him. Stepping onto the deck, the wind caught him, rustling his suit and hair. Sunnell never looked back, walking down the steps, past the end of the sidewalk, through the grass, and finally climbing onto the rock wall at the edge of the drop.

The guards waited at the end of the sidewalk, watching him.

I wanted to yell, to tell him not to jump, to run, anything else. But something held me back.

"This is wrong," I heard Megan sob. "Why is he doing this?"

I wanted to look at her, but I couldn't look away from Sunnell. One moment, he was standing on the wall, his back to us, staring out at the valley below.

Then he took a step and was gone.

Behind me, I heard Megan's sobbing increase, but I didn't turn back to see her. I just stared at the spot where Sunnell had disappeared from view. The guards had walked to the wall, and one of them bent over the edge, staring down into the darkness. I wondered if he could see Sunnell, far below.

Then I was hit with the urge to go push the guard, to send him flying over the edge, too.

"The game will resume tomorrow night," I heard Daiyu say. There was a soft sliding noise and I turned to see the dealer moving the pot from the center of the table to my spot. Across the room, I saw Daiyu disappearing down the same hall I'd emerged from. Jack and Megan were still in their chairs, Jack with his arms around the young woman as she cried. When he saw me looking, he winked at me.

What the fuck? Was this just a game to him? Did he not realize someone had lost their life because of a deck of cards, the hand they'd been dealt? I wanted to reach across the table and smack him, to send him tumbling out of his chair to the floor.

Instead, I left my chair and went to my room. Going to the bar, I uncorked the bourbon and took a swig straight from the bottle.

The alcohol burned going down my throat, but couldn't extinguish the thoughts running through my mind.

Fuck this place.

Fuck this game.

Fuck Daiyu.

I collapsed onto the couch and took another swig from the bottle, with no intention of stopping until it was empty.

5

- -

MY HEAD HURT.

I opened my eyes, then immediately closed them.

It was too damn bright.

My head hurt more.

I wanted water.

A lake, to bury my head in and drink until the headache was gone.

Fuck.

No more alcohol.

Then I remembered why I'd been drinking.

Opening my eyes, I stared at the minibar. A full bottle of bourbon had replaced the one I'd drunk from last night. That bottle was—I looked down at my hand, still grasping the neck of the bottle—empty.

Well, there were a few dregs sloshing around the bottom, but not enough to pretend I hadn't gotten drunk off my ass after watching Bob walk off the cliff.

I looked at the full bottle again, realizing it meant someone had been in my room while I slept. As a light sleeper, that surprised me. I really must have been drunk not to have heard them.

My watch beeped, and I saw it was three in the afternoon.

Five hours until tonight's game.

I needed to sober up, to get into some kind of shape to be able to compete tonight.

Fuck.

Deciding on a bath, I got to my feet as someone knocked on the door. I wasn't sure if I wanted company, but I figured it might be important. Walking over, I pulled the door open to find Megan standing there, holding a bedsheet over her naked body.

Our eyes met, and I saw the brain behind her eyes calculating, trying to decide how to take advantage of this encounter.

I shut the door before she could speak, and went to the bathroom.

A leisurely soak in the tub did wonders, and when I came back into the living room, I saw a menu had been slid under the door.

I scanned the list. Steak, chicken, fish; it sounded like airline food. But I was hungry. There was a phone on the counter, and I picked it up and punched the extension marked "Kitchen."

"Good afternoon," a voice on the other end said.

"Can you do a ribeye, medium rare, with fries and a salad, ranch dressing?" I asked.

"Of course," the voice replied. "We'll have it right to you, Sam."

I hung up before realizing I'd never told them my name.

Fuck. Maybe it was my lingering hangover, but I couldn't help but be impressed.

I was using the fries to sop up the last of the steak's juices when there was another knock at my door. Wishing it had a peephole, I cracked it, hoping I wouldn't find Megan waiting.

It was Jack. I opened the door and he came inside.

"Hot damn, Sam, you gotta get a piece of Megan before you die. It was better than my second honeymoon!"

I shook my head. "Jesus."

"Hey," he shrugged. "The condemned should enjoy their last few days." He nodded at my empty plate. "I see you're practicing for your last meal."

"You seem awfully confident," I said.

Jack laughed. "The competition ain't that strong, man. I took ten thousand off you in the last two weeks, and Megan isn't all that smart, thinking taking me to bed would give her an edge. The only one I can't figure is Daiyu."

"She's survived four of these," I reminded him. "Hosted three, and then she'd have won the first one before she hosted."

"Yeah, yeah," Jack waved his hand, then reached for the menu on the counter. "Think they'd make me a burger? I'm starving."

I gestured to the phone. "Call them and see."

"While I do, will you make me a rum and Coke?" he asked as he picked up the phone. I took a can of Coke from the fridge and a cup off the counter. Adding ice to the cup, I poured in some cola, then went to the bar. Opening the rum, I poured a healthy dose into the cocktail, at least a triple, before handing it to Jack.

He drained it in a gulp, then handed it back to me. "Another?"

I nodded, pouring more Coke in the glass, then adding as much rum as I had before. Jack sat down at the table, and I took the seat next to him. With two of these drinks in him, he'd be plenty mellow in a couple hours when the game started.

"Ain't nothing like sex and alcohol," he said, taking another swig of his cocktail. "You know you make your drinks backwards, right?"

I shrugged. "I'm not a bartender, I never learned a right way to make a drink. Besides, it all goes to the same place."

"Damn straight!" Jack took another sip of his drink. I grabbed the rum bottle and topped up his glass. He nodded appreciatively at me. "My last wife didn't like me drinking. As soon as she got me weaned off the stuff, I started thinking clearly and wondered why I put up with her."

I shook my head. "Jack, you're gonna be drunk off your ass tonight."

He laughed. "I play better drunk. Once I started drinking again, I got on a hot streak that ain't stopped. And I'm going to ride it straight to the top in this tournament."

I thought about Sunnell disappearing off the ledge. "Seems like Sunnell started at the top too."

Jack waved his hand. "Shit. He played stupid, and you accommodated him." He leaned across the table. "I don't play stupid, Sam."

"If you say so." I topped off his drink again, then went to answer the knock at the door.

"Jack's burger," one of the guards announced.

"How did you know he was here?" I asked, taking the tray.

The guard smiled. "Cameras, sir. We know everything that happens in this house, even the size of your dick."

I kicked the door closed. Fuckers. The only way they could know that was if they had cameras in the bathroom.

A bunch of perverts is what they were.

Jack grinned when I sat the burger in front of him. "Hot damn, I could get used to living like this."

"Every move you make being watched?" I asked. "Your life never more than a bad hand from ending?"

Jack took a bite of his burger. "Shit. Your life is always a moment or two from ending, you just never know when that moment is. I've scraped and scrimped through fifty-eight years, now I figure I'll enjoy a little luxury before I go."

I shook my head. "This isn't what I call luxury. It's a prison, as sure as anything. But if thinking it's a luxury helps you sleep at night, you keep thinking that. To me, it feels like I'm a condemned man in a foreign prison, one of the ones where they jump out with a gun one day and BANG! You're gone."

Jack reached out and patted my arm. "Don't worry. You won't have to live like this for long." Grabbing a fry, he popped it in his mouth. "I'll be sure to drink a toast to you every so often. Keep your memory alive, you know?"

"What if you don't survive," I asked, and saw his face darken for a bare moment.

Then he recovered, the grin reappearing. "I don't think I'll have to worry about that."

6

ONE OF THE CHAIRS had been removed, leaving four seats at the table. I took my seat to the right of the dealer, and waited for the others to join.

"Would you like something to drink?" one of the guards asked.

"Unsweet tea with lemon." His eyes showed his surprise; apparently he wasn't expecting a non-alcoholic drink. I recognized him as the one who'd leaned over the wall to look for Sunnell's body in the darkness.

I still wished I'd pushed him.

"Tell me something," I said, after he used his radio to pass my order to the kitchen. "How do you get rid of the bodies?"

"What?"

"The bodies. You can't leave a smashed corpse lying at the bottom of the cliff for someone to find. So what do you do with it?"

The guard nodded, understanding the question. "We retrieved his remains, and put them in lye. It breaks down the bodies, leaving only fragile bone fragments. After we crush them, we scatter them to the wind." A shrug. "No evidence left behind."

I looked him up and down. He was probably thirty, blonde hair pulled back in a ponytail. "How long have you been doing this?"

"This is my twelfth tournament," he replied.

"And before?"

A smile. "I ran with a German gang. The law was closing in, but a friend reached out with this opportunity, and I got out just before the Bundespolizei raided our hideout."

"So you've moved up in the world of crime?"

I'd hoped this might rattle him, and that his response might reveal something I could take advantage of. But he kept his cool. "The pay is good, and the risk is low. Your sponsors take very good care of us."

A door opened, and I turned to see Jack walking toward the table, followed by Daiyu.

"Well," I said, turning back to the guard. "It's been good talking to you..."

"Fred," he finished. "The guards are all called Fred."

"Like all the Pullman porters used to be called Jonathan," I said.

"Exactly." He smiled before stepping back.

I understood the usefulness of the method. At the turn of the twentieth century, the Black porters who worked in Pullman sleeping cars were all called "Jonathan" to save passengers the trouble of having to remember their names.

But there was a difference here. By giving all the guards the same name, it created a barrier between us and them. They were, like the porters had been, a convenience; only the guards were convenient for our sponsors, not us.

Megan joined us, wearing a low-cut top and cutoffs. Jack, I was surprised to see, had changed into a suit.

He saw me looking and winked. "She's crazy about a sharp-dressed man."

Megan reached out and put her hand on his, then looked at me. With her left eye, she winked, sending me a subtle message. *You can have this too.*

I turned to the dealer, who had just arrived, watching as she opened and shuffled a new deck. Behind her, Daiyu was playing with a chip, passing it across and between her fingers while she waited.

Fred set my tea next to me, then took drink orders from the others. The dealer chip was in front of Jack now, and the dealer looked at him.

"Hell, everyone up for some Hold 'em?"

I nodded, putting on my sunglasses. They kept people from seeing my eyes, the *windows to the soul*, they're called. I'm very good at controlling my emotions, even showing some false ones on occasion, but I still wore sunglasses.

Sometimes the best offense is a pretend defense.

"Tonight's departure method is shooting," Daiyu announced.

Jack shook his head. "That's bad news for one of you."

I picked up my cards, then laid them back on the table. The king of diamonds and the six of hearts. Tossing in the ante, I settled in as Megan checked. I added a twenty-five to the pot, just to see what people would do.

Daiyu folded, followed by Jack. Megan studied me, then tossed in twenty-five of her own.

"You can't buy the pot that cheaply," she said.

I shrugged. "All donations are welcome."

As the game went on, I found myself getting more comfortable. No matter the stakes, this was poker, a game I had played for most of my life. I was surprised how easy it was to push aside the doubt and fear and focus on the hand in front of me.

Jack was pulling ahead, up almost a thousand on the night. Five hundred of that was mine, and the other half was mostly Daiyu's. He'd clipped a little off Megan, but it was clear he was also playing to protect her.

He wanted to really enjoy that bed before she died.

The next hand began. Megan was the designated dealer, and she chose to play Draw poker. I ante'd, then took my cards and studied them. Nothing special, the ace of diamonds, a jack, seven, five, and two.

We all checked the first bet.

I took three, keeping the ace and jack. Daiyu took three, Jack took two, and Megan took three.

Looking across the table, I saw something between Jack's shirt cuff and the sleeve of his suit jacket. It looked like the edge of a playing card.

So he had something up his sleeve. Interesting.

I'd picked up another jack, along with a six and a five, so I tossed a fifty into the pot. Daiyu matched, and the bet went to Jack.

"I like this hand, so it'll cost you to stay in," he said with a grin. "See your fifty and raise you a hundred."

Megan folded, and I studied my cards for a minute. I'd seen Jack bluff before, but this was different. He was confident, sure he had something.

Maybe whatever was up his sleeve.

"Fold," I said, laying down my cards.

Daiyu looked at her hand, then pushed all her chips into the pot. "All in," she announced.

"If you insist," Jack replied, picking out the chips to match her wager. "I'll miss you."

Daiyu smiled as she laid three tens on the table. "You're a poor bluffer."

I was watching Jack's hands, and saw the move. A card slid out of his sleeve, replacing one in his hand.

"Then it's a good thing I'm not bluffing." He laid his cards on the table: three aces.

Spades, hearts, and diamonds.

As he reached for the pot, I grabbed his wrist, feeling the cards hidden up his sleeve. "You won't get away with murder that easily."

He jerked his hand away, and the approaching Freds stopped. "What the fuck are you talking about?" Jack demanded.

I flipped over my discard, the ace of diamonds on top. "Check his right sleeve," I instructed.

One of the Freds grabbed him. "Get your hands off me!" Jack demanded, trying to twist loose. Another Fred pulled a handheld taser and zapped Jack in the side. Jack's eyes went wide, and a wet spot appeared on the front of his pants as his body went slack. The Fred I'd talked to earlier reached into Jack's sleeve and pulled out four cards.

Two more aces, and the eight and seven he'd replaced with aces.

"I didn't know," Megan said, and I turned to look at her. She flipped over her cards, revealing an unimpressive hand. "He told me he was going to win, but he didn't say he was going to cheat!"

"Shut up," Jack gasped.

"He said he'd squeeze my leg under the table if he had a strong hand, so I'd know not to bet, but that's all!" She was crying now, realizing the closest thing she had to a friend had been running a hustle on the side.

Daiyu pulled in the pot and smiled. "We'll split the rest of his bank three ways."

"What?" Jack looked confused.

"You cheated," Daiyu said. "And you were caught. As punishment, you must depart."

Two of the Freds grabbed Jack and pulled him toward the door as he struggled. "This isn't right! You fuckers are mad I'm fighting for my life! Damn you all, damn you Sam!" The door closed behind them, drowning out his words as the Freds hauled him to the center of the patio. Jack looked at me, his eyes pleading, as he was forced to his knees and my Fred put a pistol to the back of his head.

Looking him in the eye, I raised my glass as Fred pulled the trigger.

7

- -

I'D BEEN IN MY room just long enough to pour a drink when someone banged on my door. Again regretting the lack of a peephole, I cracked it open, only for Megan to throw her weight against it.

"You killed him!" she yelled. As she moved back to push again, I slammed the door closed, twisting the deadbolt. Megan started banging on the door, and I walked back to the couch. "He promised to protect me, that we'd both survive, and now that can't happen!" she wailed through the door. I took a sip of my drink.

John Wayne said it best. "Life's tough. It's tougher when you're stupid." If Megan thought Jack had any intention of sacrificing himself for her when push came to shove, she'd have gotten a nasty surprise.

"Open up, you fucking asshole!" she yelled through the door. I turned on the TV. College football, two middling midwestern schools playing on a weeknight to give the network something to show. The kids playing had big dreams, but no chance of realizing them.

Kind of like us, I decided. Even if I won the tournament, what would I really gain but another tournament, another fight for my life?

Outside, the banging and yelling continued, so I cranked the volume, hoping Megan would get the hint.

She didn't.

Guilt was combining with grief. She was guilty because she'd denied Jack to avoid being labeled a cheat like him. Then she had to watch him get shot, and since she didn't want to blame herself, she'd shifted the blame to me.

It was a fucking mess, but not one I had to deal with on top of my other problems, like being trapped and playing poker for my life.

"No! Don't touch me!" Megan screamed from outside. I muted the TV and heard the electric sizzle of a taser.

Then silence.

I turned the sound back on and settled in to watch the game.

I'd just ordered a late supper when someone knocked at my door. I knew it wasn't Megan; this knock was hesitant, demure. Cracking the door, I saw Daiyu in the hall, wearing a red tank top and plaid pajama bottoms.

No bra, I noticed.

I opened the door wider. "I trust you're not here to berate me for killing your lover?"

She smiled, the first time I'd seen her do that. Her smile was pretty, almost warm, except for her eyes. They were dead.

I figured after all the people she'd seen killed, I could understand that.

Daiyu stepped past me into the room, walking to the couch. I closed the door and followed, sitting at the opposite end.

"I'm surprised to see you here," I said. "You've kept mostly to yourself."

She shrugged. "I wasn't sure about you. Tonight, I learned. You called out your friend, knowing he'd be dead because of it."

"What does that mean?" Jack wasn't really my friend, but I was more interested in her answer than correcting her.

Daiyu scooted closer, looking up at me. "It means you're a survivor."

I nodded. "Sounds about right."

She smiled. "In forty-eight hours, one of us will be dead. I think we should die happy."

I shook my head. "And you mean to tell me your charms are more enjoyable than the woman whose tits have been hanging out since we got here?"

"My previous partners have never complained. But since Megan has been sedated due to her outburst, I'm your only option at the moment." A raised eyebrow. "If you're interested, that is."

I leaned down, inhaling the scent of her perfume. It was subtle: faint, but alluring. A moment later, our lips were pressed against each other's.

My hand slid under her tank top, and I heard a soft moan. I moved it around to her back, pulling Daiyu against me.

Our kiss broke for a moment. "I want you, I want this," she whispered.

A doubt rushed through my mind. With Megan in her current state, I was Daiyu's last real competition. This was probably gamesmanship, an attempt to get inside my mind and affect my play.

Her small hand grabbed my stiff cock over my jeans, and I decided I didn't care. I removed her tank top, revealing flat, firm breasts, her small, dark nipples standing erect.

She swung her leg across my lap, straddling me as I leaned to take her left breast in my mouth. Daiyu moaned, then gently pulled away.

"Take off your clothes," she ordered, getting to her feet and dropping her pajama pants to reveal she hadn't been wearing anything underneath.

My clothes were soon abandoned, and Daiyu took my hand and led me to the bedroom.

She pushed me onto the bed, then climbed on top, straddling me. I could see the dark hair of her sex as Daiyu positioned herself, then took my cock inside her.

Jack was right about one thing: these beds were great for sex.

When we finished, Daiyu lay down next to me, her head on my arm.

"I don't know how much longer I can do this," she whispered.

I chuckled. "Was I that good?"

She shook her head, but smiled. "No, these tournaments. When I started, I had a goal, a purpose. But now I know the promises I was given were lies, and I'll never get what I want."

"Fame and fortune?"

"My daughter."

I rolled on my side, and saw a tear in Daiyu's eye. "I'm from Macau. Her father is a Chinese official. He took her back to the mainland and blocked me from crossing the border." She sniffed, and I put an arm around her. "It's been four years since I last saw her. He has power and he uses it."

"I'm sorry," I said.

"They told me if I won, they'd get her back for me. So I did. Then they told me I needed to win another, then another. Now I know it's all lies, but I'm stuck here, holding onto a glimmer of hope that one day, the lies will end."

She buried her head in my chest. The cynical part of me wondered if this was an act, but my heart was moved. It was a hell of a story, touching yet realistic. I wanted to believe Daiyu, to help reunite her with her daughter.

But I still had doubts.

I woke in the darkness to find the bed next to me empty. Sitting up, I saw a shadow moving through the room.

"Sneaking out?" I asked.

She tripped over the trays we'd set on the floor. When they finally brought my steak, there'd been one for Daiyu too. They'd been watching, and knew when we'd taken a break.

"Sorry," Daiyu said, sitting on the bed. "I was having trouble sleeping. It's been a long time since I shared a bed with anyone."

I smiled in spite of myself. If it was a lie, a manipulation, it was a good one. Make me feel special, like the only one she'd given herself to, and in a close call, I'd be like putty in her hands.

"It's okay," I said, climbing out of bed and padding to the bathroom.

When I returned, she was gone.

8

THE FRED WHO SHOT Jack brought my breakfast the next afternoon.

"A note from your sponsor." He nodded toward a piece of paper folded on the tray.

"Thank you." I took the tray and set it on the table, then reached for the note.

Opening it, I saw a simple message typed out.

Daiyu doesn't have a daughter.

I leaned back in the chair. So it had been gamesmanship, an attempt to earn sympathy. It might have worked, if we'd found ourselves in a showdown where it was her against me. But now that I knew, I had the upper hand.

I was about to throw the note away when I saw a second message hand-written at the bottom of the page.

Watch the dealer.

That was interesting. But I was hungry. Pulling the cover off the tray, I dug into my breakfast: a country ham steak, eggs over easy, hash browns, cheese grits, and toast.

A post-breakfast soak in the jacuzzi tub would help me figure out what to do with the new information, I decided as I chewed on a bite of eggs.

When I arrived at the table, a piece of paper was waiting at my spot.

Chip tally, beginning of night three:

Sam- 1,875

Daiyu- 1,600

Megan- 1,525

It was neck and neck. Only three hundred and fifty chips separated me from Megan.

At the bottom of the paper was a note.

A search of Jack's room revealed several decks of cards and other inks, dyes, and devices associated with cheating. We remind you that being caught cheating will result in your immediate departure.

"Something to drink?"

My Fred had appeared while I was reading the note. It was funny I was thinking of him that way, but he did seem to keep popping up. "I'll take a chocolate milkshake and french fries," I said, as Daiyu took her seat across the table from me.

"Martini, Fred," she said, smiling at me. Daiyu was wearing a low-cut blouse, revealing enough of her cleavage to cause a stirring in my groin.

"Hey stranger," she said, smiling at me.

Megan walked into the room topless. Daiyu and I both stared.

"What?" she yelled. "If I don't have a shirt, you can't accuse me of having something up my sleeve!"

Her breasts were even bigger than I had thought, large pink areolas in the centers of full hangers. The stirring in my groin increased.

"This isn't strip poker," I heard Daiyu say.

"Shut up, you slant-eyed whore!" Megan stomped to her seat and sat. "Well? Let's play!"

"You owe her an apology," I said, looking her in the eye. My erection was gone, replaced with anger at the slur.

"Fuck you!" She leaned across the table toward me. "I needed you last night, and you slammed the door in my face. Then I turned on my TV and saw you two going at it!"

"What?" I looked across the table at Daiyu, who was blushing.

"Yeah, all the security cameras, we can see the feeds on our TVs. Didn't your little bitch tell you that during her sob story?"

I felt myself blushing too. Even though I knew people were watching, learning how easy it was for someone to see my night with Daiyu still made me feel embarrassed.

"Put on a shirt," I finally told her.

"No." She slumped back in her chair, crossing her arms over her breasts.

"Tonight's departure is fire," Daiyu said, ignoring Megan. "If she's the loser, she'll simply crisp faster."

I noticed the temperature dropping as the night went on. Goosebumps had broken out on Megan's bare skin, and her nipples were erect from the chill. Apparently one of the Freds was manipulating the thermostat. I found myself becoming excited in spite of what Megan had said earlier.

Maybe I could punish her filthy mouth.

I kept an eye on the dealer, but it was almost midnight before I caught on to what she was doing. I'd picked Hold 'em as the game, and as she dealt out the hand, she slid cards off the bottom of the deck to Daiyu.

I was up a hundred or so from where I'd started the night, but Daiyu was up almost five hundred. Every time it seemed like Daiyu was about to lose a hand, the card she needed would appear.

And now I knew how.

Daiyu opened by betting a hundred, and Megan matched it. I tossed my cards on the table. "I got nothing. If you'll excuse me, I need to visit the little gamblers' room."

One of the Freds was in the hall, and I gestured for him to follow me toward my room.

"Do you have a camera on the dealer?" I asked.

He nodded. This Fred was built like a barrel, all of five-foot-five, but fully muscled.

"Check it," I said. "I just watched her deal to Daiyu off the bottom of the deck."

His eyes widened, and he reached for his radio as I turned to go into my suite to use the bathroom.

#

When I returned to the main room, Megan was crying.

"You shouldn't have gone all in," Daiyu taunted, raking in the pot. "I may be a slant-eyed whore, but I'm damn good at cards!"

"Because you cheat," I said, returning to my seat.

She froze for a moment. "How dare you?" she finally demanded. "You think because it worked last night, it'll work again? We're going to watch this bitch burn, then tomorrow, I'll finish you off too!"

The Fred I talked to in the hall entered the room. He walked up behind Megan. When she heard his footsteps, she shivered, and her sobbing got louder. Stopping behind her chair, he took out his pistol, raised it, and shot the dealer.

Blood, brains, and bone exploded from the back of her head onto the window, creating a gruesome splatter on the glass. For a moment, the dealer remained standing, a new hole just above her left eye. Then she collapsed to the floor, hitting her head on the table as she fell.

"The fuck was that for?" Daiyu demanded.

Fred nodded at me. "He was right. You and the dealer were cheating."

"I was not!" Daiyu shot back. "It's not my fault if she cheated!"

"She was in your room last night," Fred said. "You traded sex for favors."

My jaw dropped. "No wonder you were in such a hurry to leave last night!"

"Sam, please," she scoffed. "It's all lies."

"I know what I saw," I said as two more Freds emerged and walked toward Daiyu.

She saw the Freds approaching, and her defenses crumbled. "No! No, you can't! No!" She looked at me. "What about my little girl?"

I shook my head. "She's not real."

Daiyu's jaw dropped, then she reached into her bra and pulled out a picture. She threw it on the table as the Freds grabbed her and dragged her outside.

I reached for the image. It showed Daiyu with a little girl, a toddler, barely old enough to walk.

Fuck.

I'd believed a lie.

I looked down at the dealer's body, then outside at Daiyu. A man with a flamethrower was walking toward her. She'd been handcuffed to a metal pole planted in the ground. The flame ignited, reaching out from the wand and hitting her abdomen.

Her mouth opened in a scream, but I couldn't hear it through the thick glass.

I heard the sound of vomiting, and knew it was Megan. Footsteps echoed in the room as she ran for a toilet, but I couldn't look away, watching as Daiyu's tan skin turned black under the heat of the flame, her scream not stopping until she bowed her head and her body went limp.

The Fred running the flamethrower extinguished it and walked away, leaving Daiyu's charred body strapped to the pole.

He'd avoided her face, and I could see the stains in her makeup from the tears that had flowed down her cheeks in her final moments.

I picked the picture up and carried it outside. Daiyu's dress had been burned away, but there was a black hole in the center of her chest.

I put the picture there, close to where her heart had been. The residual heat claimed it, melting the image into Daiyu for all eternity.

9

I LAY IN BED, staring up at the ceiling.

My sponsor had lied about Daiyu's daughter.

Of course he did. She's won four straight tournaments, and he's been losing money. He saw you getting attached and took care of the problem.

The picture haunted me. In it, Daiyu's eyes had been full of life, unlike any time I'd seen her this week, and the little girl was an angel. I felt bad that Daiyu was dead.

But not that you called her out for cheating. After Jack got it last night, it was damn foolish.

Maybe she thought she'd slip under the radar, that after Jack was caught, people wouldn't be paying as close attention.

That was fucking stupid.

How long did she get away with it?

How many others died because she cheated?

A knock at the door interrupted my thoughts. I knew who it was.

There was only one person left it could be.

I thought about not answering, leaving Megan alone with her thoughts, but I decided against it.

I didn't want to be alone either.

Pulling open the door, I found her dressed in a white button-down blouse and jeans.

"Can we talk?" She asked, looking up and down the hall.

"Sure." I swung the door open to let her in.

"Thanks," she said, sitting on the couch. The same spot Daiyu had taken last night, I realized. "I just don't want to be alone tonight."

"Me either." I walked to the mini bar. "Something to drink?"

She nodded. "There should be Bloody Mary mix in your fridge."

I laughed. "Say it two more times, maybe she'll turn up and get some of these assholes along with us."

Megan smiled as I opened the refrigerator and found the cocktail mix. Pouring it in a glass with ice, I added a healthy portion of vodka from the bar and stirred before I handed it to Megan.

"You ready for tomorrow?" I asked, pouring myself a bourbon on the rocks. It was at least a triple. The "branch" in my preferred cocktail had disappeared over the cliff with Sunnell on the first night.

She shook her head. "I think I'm going to go all in on the first hand like that other guy did. I've got a fifty-fifty shot of living, which isn't bad."

I sat down on the other end of the couch and shook my head. "I'll fold."

She looked at me, her eyes widening as she realized we would both have to participate for her plan to work. "Why?" Megan finally asked.

"I couldn't live with myself if I won," I said. "If we play, me versus you, and I win on skill, I can tell myself you died because you weren't as good as me. It's a crutch, but it's a crutch I'll need."

"You can't live knowing you survived on luck," she said.

"That's right."

She looked at me for a moment, then took a sip of her Bloody Mary. "I guess that makes sense."

I shrugged. "Right now. I'm worn thin. I've just watched my third execution in three days, and tomorrow I play poker for my life. Even if I win, I'm stuck in a cycle of win or be killed for the rest of my life, however long that is."

Megan nodded. "That's the kind of stress that makes you think straight."

"You sound like you've been there before."

She nodded. "I was eighteen when I left home. My parents are Mormons; they thought I was going on my mission. But I was done with the church, done with Dad's rules, done with his hypocrisy. He was some high-ranking person in the church and acted all kind and humble when he was out in public. At home, he was completely different. If we weren't perfect, we were yelled at, beaten, whatever he felt like doing that day."

"Holy shit," I said, taking a sip of my drink.

She nodded. "We were supposed to be perfect children. So the first chance I got, I took the money I'd saved for my mission and went to Nevada. I knew prostitution was legal there, because some of the guys in my class had gone over to celebrate turning eighteen. So I found a whorehouse, passed my health test, and went to work."

"Why'd you decide on prostitution?" I asked.

She gestured at her breasts. "You saw my moneymakers tonight."

I chuckled. "You do have a point."

Megan shook her head. "I hope I gave those rich fucks a show, wherever they're hiding."

"I enjoyed it."

She smiled. "You could have fooled me."

I shrugged. "I'm a poker player. You saw my poker face."

She finished her drink, and got up to make another.

"Was that the only reason?" I asked when she sat back down.

"No," she said, shaking her head. "I figured it would embarrass the hell out of my dad if he found out what I was doing. About a month after I started, I had some flyers printed up, with real scandalous pictures, and mailed them to everyone who donated to my mission fund." Megan grinned. "Imagine if you thought you were opening some teenager's update on her mission and got a face full of girl-on-girl action instead?"

I laughed. "You probably caused a few heart attacks."

"And some broken marriages." She grinned. "I had a lot of old friends come visit, at two-hundred dollars an hour. It got so embarrassing for my dad, hearing people talk about me, that he came looking for me. But he wouldn't pay, so the bouncer kicked him out."

"So how'd you end up gambling?"

"I was in a car accident. Two broken legs, some other problems. Obviously, I wasn't much use as a sex worker, but I could sit at a poker table." Megan grinned. "By the time I was healed up, I'd turned the ten thousand left in my mission fund into a hundred thousand. Getting to pick who I fucked was another incentive." She said it cooly, but the outline of hardening nipples appeared under her shirt.

"So why'd you come east?"

"I wanted to start over. People from my hometown were still coming to look for me, some to try to 'save me,' others for physical pursuits, but I knew outside the whorehouse, I'd have to face my father if he turned up again. So I headed for the gulf coast, then made my way here."

I looked at her, and realized she had more control than she'd let on at times. I couldn't help but wonder how much of what I'd seen was an act, if she was really interested in riding Jack to victory, or if she'd been stringing him along so he wouldn't expect the dagger in his back. She'd even worn down my defenses.

"So what now?" I asked.

She slid down the couch to me. I pulled her head toward mine and kissed her, slowly at first, but then pushing my body against hers until she fell back onto the couch. I followed her down, lying on top of her, pressing my hard dick against her as I slid my hand under her shirt, caressing her breast, running my fingertip over and around her hard nipple to draw a soft moan.

"Do you really want me?" she whispered, breaking the kiss for a moment.

"I can't think of anything else I'd rather do."

10

MEGAN WAS STILL THERE when I woke up.

Sunlight came through the window, bathing her in a soft glow. The blanket had slid down, leaving the bare skin of her back exposed. She looked peaceful, content.

If I survived and she didn't, I wanted to remember her like this.

Of course, I'd also remember last night, her breasts bouncing as she rode on top of me, the moment of ecstasy as I filled her with my cum. It was something that never would have happened without this tournament: old, worn-out me fucking a smoking-hot woman half my age.

But I found myself glad it happened.

I wrapped my arms around Megan, and she leaned back into me.

"Good morning," I whispered. Finding her breast, I caressed it and heard her chuckle.

"Jesus, at least let me wake up first," she said.

I laughed. "I'm better than coffee."

"You're better than a lot of things." Megan pressed her body against mine, her bare skin warm and soft. "So last night, you got my life story. Now it's your turn."

"Seriously?"

"Yup."

I sighed. "It's pretty boring."

Megan laughed. "And mine wasn't?"

"Well, there are other activities we could partake in." I gave her breast another squeeze. She rolled over and kissed me.

"Tell me the story, then we'll consider other options."

"Okay," I sighed. "I retired from the Coast Guard."

"Oooh," she smiled. "A military man."

I laughed. "Not really. I was a telephone technician. Anyway, I'm leaving my retirement party with no idea what I want to do or where I want to go, driving south on I-5 north of Seattle, when I see I sign for a casino. I decide, 'What the hell, I've got a couple grand,' so I go in and find a poker table. Two weeks later, I was still there. I started moving from place to place, exploring America and gambling, trying to decide on my next step." I shrugged. "That was seven years ago, and I'm still trying to decide."

"And you wound up here," Megan said, tracing her fingers across my chest.

"So did you."

"And tonight, one of our adventures ends," Megan whispered. "I've been lonely for a long time, since before I left home. Even with Jack, it was transactional; he wanted me for my body, I wanted him for the protection he offered. But last night..." She chuckled. "If you told me when I walked in with my shirt off that I'd fall asleep in your arms, I'd have laughed in your face. But last night, telling you my story, falling asleep with you, I didn't feel alone for the first time I can remember."

I gulped. "I know what you mean. My parents died right after I enlisted. I was married once, years ago, but it didn't last. I've had friends, girlfriends, but when it comes down to it, I've mostly been a drifter."

"I think that's how most gamblers live. Even in the old west, they always seemed to end up alone."

I nodded, pulling her even closer. Her smell, her shampoo, everything about her, I never wanted to let go.

And soon I'd be playing cards to try to kill her.

"What's your last request?" I asked.

"What?" She looked surprised.

"The way I see it, we're both condemned. We'll have us a good last meal, but outside of that, what's your last request?"

Megan thought for a moment. "I want someone to tell me they love me and mean it," she said. "I've heard the words, but it's never been backed up by action."

God, I hadn't heard or said those words since my failed marriage. I was out of practice, for sure.

She leaned in and kissed me. "No fair saying it now."

I nodded.

"What about you," she asked.

"I want this fucking tournament ended," I said. "I want everyone responsible for it to depart, in the same ways we've seen people depart over the last few days."

Megan smiled. "Maybe we can both get what we want."

I kept silent, not daring to hope for what I really wanted. Who knew you could fall for someone in a matter of hours, to completely change how you saw them once you understood what made them how they were? I wanted to spend a lifetime with Megan, but I dared not hope for it.

I'd settle for ending the tournament.

"Good evening."

I recoiled in shock when I saw who the dealer was. Beside me, Megan squeezed my hand hard.

Andy Whitmer, the asshole responsible for recruiting us with lies and promises, stood behind the table.

"Surprised?" he asked, and we approached the table. "After the unfortunate incident with the last dealer, the sponsors insisted on someone they trust absolutely."

I fingered the paring knife I'd stuck in my pocket before I left my room. I didn't know why I'd done it, and I hadn't expected to have an opportunity to use it, but looking at Whitmer, I knew I'd use it if he gave me a chance.

"Tonight's departure method is beheading," he announced as Megan and I took our seats.

"If we wanted a demonstration, could they lop off your head?" I asked.

Whitmer laughed. "I'm afraid not. But you'll either get a demonstration, or be part of one, before the night is over."

I looked down at my chips. Before we came in, Megan and I had agreed the poker was poker, and neither of us would try to twist it to prolong the inevitable.

Looking at Whitmer, I realized he was enjoying this. I had little doubt he'd spent the week somewhere nearby, watching things unfold through the cameras.

"You're the first dealer," he said, sliding the chip in front of Megan.

"Stud," she decided.

The last hand began around two in the morning. Megan was down to her last five hundred chips, and it was my turn as dealer. We'd talked all night, as Whitmer looked on, waiting to pounce.

I called Draw, and when I picked up my cards, I had to make a decision.

Megan bet all but a hundred, and I called the bet. She took two cards. I looked at my hand again. It hadn't changed.

"How many?" Whitmer asked.

"One," I said.

He dealt the card, and I laid my other cards on top of it. Megan pushed her last hundred chips into the pot. "I'm all in."

I added a chip of my own. Megan wasn't a bad poker player, but I was better. She'd gotten here because of Jack's protection and Daiyu's cheating, not any skill of her own.

Megan laid her cards out, looking nervous. "Three nines," she said.

I flipped my cards over. On top, the last card Whitmer had dealt me, was the ace of hearts.

Fanning my cards, I reveled in the four other hearts beneath it.

A flush.

Megn paled. Across the table, Whitmer smiled as three Freds came into the room.

Pushing my chair back, I jumped across the table, knocking Whitmer to the floor. Pulling the paring knife from my pocket, I stabbed it into his throat, pushing and pulling as blood flowed from the wound.

Strong hands grabbed me, trying to pull me off, but I knocked them away, digging the knife deeper and deeper. They grabbed me again, lifting me off, but looking at Whitmer's face, his skin whitening as the blood flowed out and pooled around his head, I knew he was dead.

"Fuck you!" I yelled.

Someone wrenched the knife from my hand. Another Fred came running with a first aid kit, but it wouldn't help.

I was glad Whitmer was dead.

Pushing the Freds aside, I ran out to the patio, where another Fred had forced Megan to kneel. He was stepping behind her, a massive sword in his hand. I started toward them, with no plan other than to get between Megan and the sword, when I was grabbed from behind.

"Megan!" I yelled. "I love you!"

She looked up at me and smiled. "I love you too."

The Fred swung the sword, and her head rolled across the deck, coming to a rest at my feet.

As I looked into her eyes, I realized I envied her fate. Soon, I'd have to do this all over again, while she'd been set free.

Maybe I wasn't the winner after all.

Acknowledgements

I learned to play poker in two places: at a monastery in South Carolina during a youth retreat, and at my grandfather's dining room table. I'm grateful for the participants at both places.

As always, thank you to Cyan and Rebecca for taking on another crazy idea and finding a way to make it work.

Thank you to my wonderful wife, Anna, for not brutally murdering me or the kids.

Thank you to my children for doing their best to distract me from finishing this novelette.

Thank you to you, dear reader. Without you, this would be another file on my computer waiting to be read.

About D.L. Winchester

D.L. Winchester lives in the foothills of southern Appalachia. A former mortician, his work searches the darkness to find tales worth telling. He is the author of over three hundred obituaries, numerous short stories, and the upcoming flash fiction collection "A Terrible Place." In his spare time, he can be found searching for inspiration in the world around him and trying to keep his children from becoming the next generation of horror villains.

UB Website

If you are a fan of horror stories and tales,
you'll want to follow Undertaker Books.
We're bringing you stories to take to your grave.

www.ingramcontent.com/pod-product-compliance
Lightning Source LLC
Chambersburg PA
CBHW030947310726
48969CB00008B/2400